Captain Scarlet

Instrument of Destruction
Parts 1 & 2

Also published by Puffin

Spectrum Agents' Handbook

Captain Scarlet
Instrument of Destruction
Parts 1 & 2

Text by Richard Dungworth

PUFFIN

PUFFIN BOOKS

Published by the Penguin Group
Penguin Books Ltd, 80 Strand, London WC2R 0RL, England
Penguin Group (USA) Inc., 375 Hudson Street, New York,
New York 10014, USA
Penguin Group (Canada), 90 Eglinton Avenue East, Suite 700, Toronto,
Ontario, Canada M4P 2Y3 (a division of Pearson Penguin Canada Inc.)
Penguin Ireland, 25 St Stephen's Green, Dublin 2, Ireland (a division of
Penguin Books Ltd)
Penguin Group (Australia), 250 Camberwell Road, Camberwell, Victoria
3124, Australia (a division of Pearson Australia Group Pty Ltd)
Penguin Books India Pvt Ltd, 11 Community Centre, Panchsheel Park,
New Delhi – 110 017, India
Penguin Group (NZ), cnr Airborne and Rosedale Roads, Albany, Auckland
1310, New Zealand (a division of Pearson New Zealand Ltd)
Penguin Books (South Africa) (Pty) Ltd, 24 Sturdee Avenue, Rosebank,
Johannesburg 2196, South Africa

Penguin Books Ltd, Registered Offices: 80 Strand, London WC2R 0RL,
England

www.penguin.com

First published 2006
1

Anderson Entertainment Ltd/GAP PLC © MMIV. Original Production
CAPTAIN SCARLET © 1967 ITC. CAPTAIN SCARLET is used under
licence by Granada Ventures Limited.

Text by Richard Dungworth

Set in Helvetica by Palimpsest Book Production Limited,
Polmont, Stirlingshire
Made and printed in England by Clays Ltd, St Ives plc

British Library Cataloguing in Publication Data
A CIP catalogue record for this book is available from the British Library

ISBN-13: 978-0-141-32048-9
ISBN-10: 0-141-32048-6

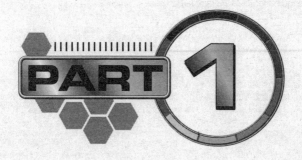

Chapter 1

Conrad Lefkon, designated Spectrum agent Captain Black, stripped off the EMR Scanner headset and turned away from the neon monitor screen. His eyes ached from staring at the glowing display. The strange screeching signals continued to ring in his head, even without the earpiece.

After two weeks of deep space travel, Black was beginning to tire of living in the shuttle's confined, zero-gravity conditions. Mars was a memorable destination, certainly, but it was a long haul. And the unexplained extraterrestrial signals that he and his crewmate, Captain Scarlet, had been sent seventy-eight million kilometres to investigate had so far proved impossible to track to a specific source – despite days of continuous monitoring.

3

Black pushed himself off from the console and drifted across the cabin.

'It's nothing but a wild goose chase, I'm telling you.' He shook his head.

He floated along the shuttle's interior using the yellow grab handles to propel himself. Scarlet was strapped to the exercise bike, beginning to wind down his cardio workout.

Not that either he or Black needed to tone up – both men were in top physical condition. Lean but muscular, 1.88 metres and black-haired, they were much alike but for their faces – Scarlet's fathomless eyes were a cool, piercing blue, while Black's were dark brown, deep-set under heavy brows.

'Some twentieth-century Russki probe gone renegade,' continued Black. 'That's what's making this noise.'

'Then why can't the scientists at the Mars base find it?' replied Scarlet, breathing heavily.

'I don't know, and I don't know how they expect us to, either.'

Scarlet's pedalling legs slowed to a halt. Releasing the handlebars, he sat upright and grabbed a towel floating an arm's length away. As he mopped his brow, he gave his fellow agent a wry smile.

'You know, Conrad, just because Spectrum designated you Black, it doesn't mean you have to be negative *all* the time.'

During his time with the Special Forces, Scarlet – or Commander Paul Metcalfe, as he had been known then – had grown accustomed to Black's droll pessimism. Black had been second in command of the elite unit led by Scarlet, and a first-class soldier. By the time they joined Spectrum, the pair had become firm friends.

'I know.' Black smirked as he floated past Scarlet and continued along the cabin towards the food and drink dispenser. 'But what are the odds the coffee's cold? Want some anyway?'

Without warning there was a sound like machine-gun fire as several small fragments of rock burst through the shuttle's side, narrowly missing Scarlet. Instantly, the cabin was thrown into chaos, becoming a maelstrom of howling wind and flying objects as the air within its pressurized interior rushed through the punctured wall into the vacuum of deep space beyond, taking with it anything that wasn't secured firmly.

'Meteor strike!' yelled Scarlet above the roaring din. He clung desperately to the exercise bike's frame, bolted to the wall, as his body flailed in the stream of rushing air. Lose his grip, he knew, and he would be sucked away into the void in a flash.

As emergency lights blinked red and the decompression alarms blared out, Black, gripping a grab handle further along the cabin, had a sudden dreadful realization. The shuttle had an automatic anti-decompression safety system which would shut the air-tight bulkhead at the end of the damaged section to prevent the entire ship from depressurizing. Black was on the safe side of this bulkhead. Scarlet wasn't.

'Decompression. Decompression,' wailed the shuttle's alarm system. 'Emergency bulkhead closing in five seconds . . . four . . . three –'

'Scarlet! Come on!' Black urged his friend to drag himself against the rushing air.

'Two . . . one –'

'Paul!' yelled Black, as the emergency bulkhead doors sliced together in an instant, sealing him in sudden calm, but leaving Scarlet beyond help.

Black knew he had only moments to rescue his friend. Even if Scarlet could maintain his handhold, he would run out of oxygen within seconds.

Thinking fast, Black pulled hard on a grab handle, sending himself sailing some six metres across the craft's interior to where the shuttle's huge planetary exploration vehicle – a Bison All-Terrain Vehicle (ATV) – was parked. A panel in the Bison's rear end read EMERGENCY EQUIPMENT. Black hit the panel's release catch and hurriedly withdrew the harness and winch from inside the compartment.

Black quickly wrapped the harness belt round his waist, attached the winch controller to its buckle and clipped the winch motor itself behind his back. Ensuring the end of the winch's cable was firmly secured, he pushed off again, floating fast to the sealed bulkhead, the cable unreeling behind him.

Conscious that he was running out of time, Black took a palm-sized Stinger explosive charge from his belt, clamped it to the joint in the bulkhead doors and hit its central trigger button. Six detonator legs shot out from the circular charge, as a neon digit in its centre counted down. 3 . . . 2 . . . 1 . . .

Black shielded his eyes from the blast, then dived through the now-open bulkhead, allowing the depressurization to pull him towards Scarlet.

Scarlet, oxygen-starved and barely conscious, still somehow clung to the exercise bike with the last shreds of his strength. As Black reached him, he wrapped both arms round Scarlet's waist and punched the winch trigger on his belt-mounted control panel. The powerful motor instantly kicked in, reeling both men out of the damaged section at high speed just moments before the emergency bulkhead doors snapped shut again.

As it fully retracted, the winch cable slammed Black's back hard against the rear of the Bison, the jolt causing Scarlet's head to whiplash against the vehicle's side.

'You OK?' asked Black, winded but unhurt, as his reviving friend rubbed the back of his skull.

Intact, but badly shaken, Scarlet looked at his fellow agent. His face was lined with concern. 'You know,' he said, 'I'm getting a bad feeling about this mission.'

The Bison ATV scuttled across the dusty red Martian landscape. This powerful and robust vehicle was the ultimate All-Terrain Vehicle, boasting the latest in both drive and suspension technology. Even the mountainous, rock-strewn surface of Mars posed little challenge for its ultra-responsive 10x10 system and tough armoured body.

Inside the pressurized cabin, Captain Scarlet looked out through the viewing window in awe as he piloted the Bison across the alien territory.

'A hellish beauty.' That was how his father had described the appearance of this remarkable but unwelcoming planet.

His father. Pioneering astronaut Commander

Tom Metcalfe who, over twenty years ago, had become the first human to set foot on Mars. Scarlet could vividly remember watching the pictures from Earth, a young boy, fiercely proud of his dad.

Scarlet suppressed the all-too-familiar pang of loss, grateful when Captain Black's voice broke his reverie.

'OK. Zone Alpha Five Two – clear.'

Black's tone betrayed his weariness. They had covered over thirty search zones since touching down in the Shuttle's Excursion Vehicle, but as yet had located no source for the unexplained signals. Black had done his best to make the surveillance scanner's display a little more appealing. A recent photo of Destiny Angel, his stunning girlfriend and ace Spectrum fighter pilot, adorned the console.

'This is like fishing in a desert,' Black grumbled.

'Well, something has to be sending that signal,' sighed Scarlet.

'So, we keep looking,' finished Black, as he punched the next set of search codes into the Bison's surveillance system.

As the Bison crested a rise, Scarlet pulled back

on the control column to bring the vehicle to a halt. Stretching out in front of them, as far as the eye could see, was a vast, featureless basin of dusty red rock.

'What a sight,' commented Scarlet, eyes wide in wonder.

Black, too, was impressed. 'I wish Destiny could have seen this,' he murmured, looking out over the breathtaking panorama.

Suddenly, he clutched his earpiece excitedly and looked down at the scanner's flashing display.

'Hey, wait – I've got a fix!'

'But – there's nothing out there,' said Scarlet, looking over at him in bewilderment.

Then, as Scarlet turned back to the viewing window, something strange began to happen. Over the entire surface of the giant depression ahead, a cloud of dust was beginning to form. As Scarlet watched, it accumulated in the basin's centre, where it rose to create a towering central pillar.

'Oh yes there is . . .' murmured Black, eyes no longer on the scanner, transfixed by what they were witnessing.

'Some kind of hologram?' suggested Scarlet, bewildered, as ghostly structures gradually became visible amid the spiralling dust.

Black glanced down. 'No – my instruments confirm it's there all right.'

Slowly, a vast civilization appeared, as though taking shape before their very eyes. Highly sophisticated structures, unlike anything Scarlet or Black had ever seen on Earth, grew around a central, awe-inspiring tower of multiple disc-like layers, somehow suspended by a column of flowing green light. Every surface and structure of the strange, vast city pulsed with streams of the same lurid green light.

When the dust veil lifted completely, the agents found their voices.

'An alien city!' Scarlet was dumbfounded. 'But there have been people on Mars for twenty years. How come no one has seen this before?'

'Maybe they didn't want to be seen,' suggested Black.

Their trance was broken by the insistent beeping of one of the Bison's alarms. A translucent, green-tinged sphere, with a bright central core, was moving rapidly from the alien city's central tower, heading straight towards the Bison.

'What is it?' snapped Scarlet.

Black hurriedly checked the system readings. 'We're picking up a huge surge of –'

Suddenly, the warning alarm stepped up in

pitch, pace and volume, and Black's screen flashed wildly.

'We're under attack!'

Before Scarlet could respond, Black's fingers danced across the Bison's weapons control touch screen. Instantly, the Bison's roof-mounted missile launcher sprang from its housing, unleashing three rocket-powered missiles which streaked towards the approaching the sphere.

After the missiles hit, the alien sphere exploded in a ball of fire. Somehow, this set off a second, larger explosion in the nearest section of the alien city. Within moments, a chain reaction of ever greater blasts had created an expanding fireball, engulfing building after building.

In the Bison, Scarlet and Black shielded their eyes from the glare as every part of the vast city before them was consumed by a rolling wave of fire. When the central tower collapsed into the inferno, there was a blinding flash, then, seconds later, total silence.

As the dust cloud settled, Scarlet and Black looked on from the Bison in shock. All trace of the city had vanished. The rocky depression before them was once again featureless and still.

*   *   *

Scarlet was first to break the eerie silence.

'What have we done?' he muttered, appalled by the enormity of the destruction the Bison's missiles had caused.

'But it was coming straight for us!' Black reminded him.

'It could have been some kind of scan.'

'Come on, Paul, what did you expect me to do – wait until we were blown to pieces before firing back?'

'We've destroyed the whole city,' murmured Scarlet to himself, unable to come to terms with what had happened.

But as he looked out once more through the Bison's viewing window, his remorse changed to astonishment, then terror. The alien city was rising from the valley floor again, just as it had before, seemingly unscathed by the cataclysmic fire.

'Not yet, we haven't!' said Black, grabbing the Bison's drive control hastily. 'Let's get out of here!'

Black threw the Bison into reverse and spun it round in a three-point turn, throwing up a cloud of red dust. Resuming control, Scarlet hit full throttle, keen to put some distance between their vehicle and the indestructible city, now fully resurrected behind them.

As the ATV hurtled across the rock-strewn terrain, bouncing wildly, a second airborne sphere emerged from the central tower of the city and began to pursue the retreating Bison. Gaining ground quickly, it began to hover lower and lower. Instead of landing on the planet's surface, the sphere simply melted into it. Merging with the rock, it transformed into a circle of green light.

The luminous green ring continued to move rapidly along the planet's surface, as though projected on to it from above. When close to the fast-moving Bison, the single glowing circle separated into two.

The twin circles finally caught the Spectrum vehicle and they played on its rear and upper surfaces, like sinister torchlights. Next the speeding vehicle was inexplicably thrown out of control.

Careering wildly off course, the Bison plummeted into a ravine, clattering down its sharp incline in a shower of boulders, before coming to an abrupt standstill, severely battered, wedged awkwardly in a rocky crevice.

Inside the ATV, Scarlet and Black had taken a battering, too, saved from serious injury only by the Bison's robust restraint harnesses.

While the two men took stock of their aches and bruises, the twin circles of green light found the crippled Bison and slunk across its battered body. They settled on the vehicle's viewing window, directly above where Black and Scarlet lay tipped back in their seats and pinned down by their restraints.

Black and Scarlet stared up at the strange rings of light above them and were bewildered to hear a deep, resonant, inhuman voice fill the Bison's cabin.

'EARTHMEN,' the disembodied voice began, 'THIS IS THE VOICE OF THE MYSTERONS. WE HAVE WATCHED YOU FOR CENTURIES. YOUR VIOLENCE DISGUSTS US. AND NOW YOU VISIT IT UPON US.'

Black and Scarlet exchanged anxious glances as the alien voice continued.

'YOU CANNOT DESTROY US, EARTHMEN. BUT NOW WE WILL CRUSH YOUR WORLD.'

When the voice's echo died away, the rings of green light started playing on the window above the men and began to glow steadily brighter. Scarlet and Black shielded their eyes from the glare as their intensity increased. Then, in a sudden rush, the rings merged into a blinding flood of intense green-white light.

Scarlet felt searing, unbearable pain as the alien light flooded his mind. He vaguely heard his friend's agonized scream blend with his own, and then he knew no more.

Chapter 3

The sleek white aircraft hugged the sparkling surface of the water as the river twisted and turned along the rocky canyon. Despite its astonishing speed, which would have been impressive even in straight flight, the plane negotiated the narrow, winding channel with ease.

But this was no ordinary jet. The Spectrum Falcon, with its twin state-of-the-art Halo Pulsejets and revolutionary aerodynamics, was the fastest and most manoeuvrable strike fighter ever built. And this particular Falcon was under the control of a truly exceptional pilot.

'Destiny Angel to Control. We're returning to base.'

Snugly installed in the cockpit, Simone Giraudoux

– or Destiny Angel, as she was officially designated – smiled to herself. The training exercise
had gone well, but she was looking forward to
getting back to Skybase, not least in order to
catch up on news of Conrad, so many millions
of kilometres away.

Despite her years as a shuttle pilot for the ISA
(International Space Agency), Mars was one
destination that Destiny had yet to visit. Part of
her envied her boyfriend the opportunity of seeing
the mysterious Red Planet for himself. Since she
had become leader of Angel Squadron, space
travel had moved way down the agenda.

Not that Destiny would have had it any other
way. Piloting ISA spacecraft had largely involved
overseeing flight computers and monitoring automated systems. Space travel was interesting –
exciting even – but flying a Falcon was something
else altogether.

In fact, Destiny sometimes couldn't quite believe
her good fortune. A year short of her thirtieth
birthday, and here she was, in what surely had to
be the best job on Earth, commanding Spectrum's
elite air-defence team, flying alongside the very
best pilots, with the ultimate jet-fighter technology
at her fingertips.

As she expertly negotiated another turn in the river canyon, Destiny checked her display for the position of her fellow Angels. Right on cue, the four white Falcons of Harmony, Melody, Symphony and Rhapsody fell in behind Destiny's lead plane in perfect V-formation.

Destiny pulled back on the Falcon's control column, pointing its nose skyward, into the sun. Holding formation, the four following planes swooped up after her. As one, the squadron roared away from the canyon, climbing rapidly towards Skybase, Spectrum's airborne head-quarters, which hovered 60,000 feet above in the clear blue sky.

As the Falcons neared the massive hovering platform, held aloft by its six huge fusion engines, Destiny reopened communications.

'Skybase, this is Destiny Angel. Approaching you from the west. Request permission to land.'

'Destiny Angel,' Lieutenant Green's familiar voice came over her helmet headset, 'you are clear to land on Runway One. Crosswind forty knots.'

'Destiny Angel, S-I-G,' Destiny confirmed as she expertly swung the Falcon into its final approach, lining up with the specified runway, one of four that criss-crossed the Flight Deck on Skybase's upper surface.

As the plane touched down, the landing shoes beneath its nose and each of its wing-tips instantly locked into the magnetic rails that ran the 330-metre length of the Magna-strip runway. These strips rapidly decelerated the aircraft, bringing it to a halt in the centre of a large circular platform at the runway's far end.

The moment the Falcon came to a standstill, the circular platform began to drop and revolve, spinning the aircraft through 180 degrees as it was lowered into the Hangar Deck below. Robotic servicing arms clamped on to the Falcon's fusel-age and began busily refuelling, rearming and cleaning the plane as it moved automatically along more Magna-strip rails towards its standby docking position.

A tall, blond-haired man, clearly of Scandinavian extraction, and wearing a blue Spectrum uniform, was waiting at the dock. Adam Svenson, desig-nated Captain Blue, had come to meet Destiny.

The Falcon pulled alongside him, stopped and its cockpit canopy slid smoothly back. Destiny Angel lifted off her flight helmet and shook out her blonde hair.

'Destiny.' Captain Blue greeted her, his tone rather flat.

'Adam.' Pleasantly surprised to be met, Destiny smiled widely at her friend, blue eyes sparkling. But as she took in his subdued look, her smile faded.

'What's wrong?'

'It's Conrad and Paul. We've . . .' Blue looked down awkwardly and Destiny felt a coldness grip her heart. 'We've lost all contact.'

Some 125 million kilometres away, in the cabin of the stranded Bison, Captain Scarlet fought to suppress the throbbing haze in his head as he gradually regained consciousness.

Massaging his sore neck, Scarlet turned his head gingerly. Black was slumped forward in his seat, still unconscious. His right arm stretched out over the control console, Destiny's photograph clutched and partially crumpled in his hand.

'Conrad!'

No longer pinned down by his safety restraint, Scarlet was able to reach across to shake Black roughly by the shoulder.

'Conrad!'

There was no response. Black showed no signs of life. And the hand that held Destiny's photograph was deathly cold.

Chapter 4

Conrad Lefkon was buried with full military honours three weeks later, in a quiet English country churchyard, far from the barren Red Planet where he had lost his life. His funeral was presided over by Sir Charles Grey, designated Colonel White, Spectrum's Supreme Commander.

White was a distinguished-looking man, 1.83 metres tall, white-haired, with intelligent blue eyes and an athletic physique that belied his fifty-five years.

Educated at Oxford University and Sandhurst Military Academy, he had gone on to become a much-decorated Royal Marine, before pursuing a career in British Military Intelligence (MI6). While serving as Director of MI6 he received his knighthood for Services to the British Empire.

But it was the horror of the Global Terrorist Wars, in which he had lost so many good friends, that spurred White on to achieve his ultimate goal – the establishment of a worldwide security network. This global security organization, championed by White during his years as head of the United Nations Security Development Committee, was now a reality. It was Spectrum.

In his various roles across his thirty-year career, White had seen too many good men lay down their lives for their beliefs. Though this was far from White's first military burial, he nevertheless felt a keen sense of loss – Black had been a decent man, and a fine agent. He would be much missed.

And for some among his fellow mourners, White realized, Black's death would bring much greater grief.

Captain Scarlet, he knew, had had his fair share of funerals. First his parents and now his best friend. The anger and pain must be unbearably familiar.

White greatly respected the way in which Scarlet dealt with his anger, channelling it into his work.

He doubted whether Scarlet would have become such an exemplary operative – perhaps Spectrum's finest – were it not for his previous terrible loss. After all, Scarlet's transfer from the US Air Force to the Special Forces, which had culminated in his Spectrum appointment, had been largely driven by his desire to avenge his parents' death.

And, of course, there was Destiny. The colonel had never met a tougher young woman, mentally or physically – she was a fearless pilot and a formidable combatant. However her happiness had been ripped apart by her boyfriend's death.

As he watched Destiny step forward to Black's coffin and tearfully lay a single red rose on top of it, White swore to himself that those responsible would be brought to justice.

Getting to grips with Spectrum's newly encountered extraterrestrial enemy was proving a hard task.

Captain Scarlet had been fully debriefed following his lonely return shuttle flight from Mars. He had recounted the events of the ill-fated mission in detail. But, in truth, there had been little he could offer by way of factual information about Earth's would-be destroyers – the enigmatic 'Mysterons'.

White had authorized the use of the full range of Spectrum's considerable technological resources in an attempt to find out more. So far, they had drawn a blank.

'The signals from Mars have stopped and there's no sign of the alien city,' explained Colonel White at an emergency briefing in his Skybase office shortly after Black's funeral. 'Nevertheless, there can be no doubt that these Mysterons pose a deadly threat to Earth's security.'

The assembled group comprised White's six top captains, including Scarlet and Blue, plus Destiny Angel. All those present knew that if the colonel was worried, there was cause for real concern. White didn't scare easily.

'Fighting an enemy we can't see!' exclaimed Captain Blue, incredulously. The burly, tall US Army veteran clearly favoured an opponent who could be grappled with.

'Or one that we *can* see, but *can't* recognize . . .' mused Captain Scarlet.

Off duty, Scarlet was resting in his quarters. Since returning from Mars, he had slept little, often waking in a cold sweat, his head filled with muddled images of Martian ravines, apocalyptic fire and Black's ashen face.

Now, as he slept fitfully, a new nightmare was about to begin.

Twin circles of lurid green light moved across the room to Scarlet's bed and crept across his prone body. Suddenly, Scarlet's hallucinations became more vivid. He moaned, and his head thrashed from side to side as something in his subconscious tried to shake the dreadful, unearthly voice that had begun to echo within it. The voice of the Mysterons.

'WE WILL CRUSH YOUR WORLD, EARTHLING. WE WILL DESTROY YOU AS YOU DESTROY YOUR OWN KIND. *YOU* WILL BE OUR INSTRU- MENT OF DESTRUCTION, CAPTAIN SCARLET.'

Sitting bolt upright on his bed, Scarlet's head lolled as though he were not yet awake. As he raised his expressionless face in the dimness of his darkened room, his eyes flashed with a lurid green light.

Captain Blue was having a quick coffee in the Observation Lounge when the alarms sounded. Not that any alarm was required to tell Blue that something was badly wrong – moments before the alert the entire base had lurched violently to one side, sending his coffee cup sliding off the table.

Skybase was stabilized by a dozen powerful thrusters, in addition to its six enormous main jets. Blue knew that only a serious malfunction could have caused such a major jolt.

He dashed out of the lounge to Central Control. As he hurriedly entered, he was greeted by even more wailing alarms.

Lieutenant Green, Colonel White's executive officer and the ultimate authority on all Skybase's ICT systems, was frantically scanning her vast control screen.

A worried-looking Colonel White sprang into life on one sector of Green's display, speaking via the video ComLink.

'Lieutenant Green – report.'

'Multiple engine failure, colonel.'

'I'll be right there.' The colonel's video image blinked off as he hurried from his quarters.

Captain Blue, in the meantime, had been checking the Engineering Deck video monitor. He was shocked at what it showed.

'It's no engine failure – it's Scarlet!'

Sure enough, on the monitor's display, Captain Scarlet could be seen in the process of shutting down one of Skybase's vital jet engines.

Blue didn't wait to watch what Scarlet planned to do next. Dashing out of Central Control, he sprinted along the corridors towards Engineering, stumbling as Skybase see-sawed again. Another jet had shut down.

Approaching the final corridor, Blue found it barred by a sealed bulkhead which two technicians were urgently trying to cut through with laser torches. Clearly Scarlet wanted Engineering to himself.

There's another way in, though, Blue remembered. He hastily pulled away an access hatch in the wall beside the bulkhead to reveal the electrical conduit and ventilation shaft behind it. Crawling into the confined space, Blue managed to make his way along into a section of ducting that protruded from the wall of the main Engineering Deck.

Peering through a ventilation grille, he could see Scarlet below, running through the sequence of actions that would deactivate another of the base's jets.

Blue grabbed his laser pistol from its thigh-holster and kicked open the grille. Scarlet looked up at the sound. His eyes flashed luminous green as he reached for his own firearm.

Blue had no choice. His well-aimed shot caught Scarlet in the chest. The force of the blast lifted Scarlet off his feet, sending him tumbling over the railings behind him. As he fell ten metres to the floor below, Scarlet passed directly through the highly charged electron plasma stream of one of the base's massive jets. Then he hit the floor and lay still.

Captain Blue jumped down from the ventilation shaft and quickly reactivated the jet being silenced by Scarlet.

With a sinking feeling, he crossed to the railings and looked down at his friend spreadeagled below. There was little chance Scarlet could have survived the impact and even less chance that contact with the plasma stream hadn't proved fatal.

Why, oh why, had Scarlet, of all people, turned saboteur?

'No obvious signs of trauma.'

Doctor Gold, head of Skybase's Medical Centre, was examining the motionless body of Captain Scarlet laid out in the centre's state-of-the-art operating theatre.

As the operating table's integral MRI scanner completed its pass, a Multi-purpose Surgical Auxiliary (MSA), suspended from the ceiling by a robotic arm, automatically swung into position over Scarlet's damaged body. Under the guidance of one of the three medics assisting Doctor Gold, the MSA moved busily over Scarlet's chest, its hypodermics injecting the necessary drugs.

As Gold struggled to save his Spectrum colleague, his commentary grew increasingly ominous.

'His stats are down.'

From the gallery behind the transparent polymer walls encasing the theatre, Destiny Angel watched and listened, desperate for a sign that Scarlet would pull through. Losing Conrad had been a wrench. But to lose Paul as well, so soon after, would be more than she could bear.

Captain Blue and Colonel White stood beside her, their faces full of concern, their expressions less than hopeful.

Gold was the best there was, Destiny knew. Skybase's silver-haired, bespectacled medic – real name Mason Frost – had multiple doctorates from the University of Vienna and George Washington University School of Medicine, as well as a well-founded reputation as one of the world's most innovative and accomplished surgeons. If anyone could save Scarlet, Gold could. Destiny would not give up hope.

One of Gold's assistants glanced anxiously at the falling readings on the vital-signs monitor beside him. 'Systolic down to ninety-eight; not looking good.'

'I know that,' Gold snapped. 'Switch on respiratory support.'

The operating theatre's ring of powerful ceiling

lights glared down on Scarlet's impassive face. His left cheek was streaked with an angry-looking electrical burn from the plasma stream.

'Pulse fading.' This from another of the assistants.

A note of despair crept into the Gold's voice. 'It's too late, we're losing him.'

Even as he spoke, the read-outs on the vital-signs monitor suddenly flattened out, the neon numerals flickering to zero, the intermittent beep that had signified Scarlet's struggle to survive becoming a single, continuous tone.

Doctor Gold, beaten, turned away from Scarlet. When he looked up at his colleagues on the gallery outside, his face, usually full of humour and energy, betrayed his anguish.

'There never was really any hope, I'm afraid.'

As Gold and his team dejectedly switched off the medical equipment and prepared to leave the theatre, Colonel White laid a comforting hand on Destiny's shoulder. The Angels' leader hung her head, bowed and broken.

With no adequate words of solace, White turned and made his way out of the Medical Centre.

'Come on, Destiny.' Captain Blue spoke gently, his voice full of compassion.

Destiny stared blankly down, inconsolable. 'Please – I need a few minutes . . .'

'Sure.'

Blue followed the colonel out of the gallery door, leaving Destiny alone.

As Destiny struggled to come to terms with this latest devastating blow, something strange was happening to Scarlet. The scorch mark on his cheek was fading rapidly. Within seconds, the damaged tissue was mysteriously replaced by healthy skin and the burn had vanished completely.

Moments later, unnoticed by the withdrawing medical staff, Scarlet's eyelids flickered open.

Lifting her head sadly to take a last look at her lost friend, Destiny, incredulous at first, saw his open eyes and waking movements.

'Doctor Gold! Doctor Gold! He's alive!'

Gold was heading for the theatre door, when Destiny's ecstatic cry and enthusiastic thumping on the transparent gallery wall above drew his attention.

Startled, the doctor turned to look at Scarlet. To his utter amazement, he saw that Destiny was right – Scarlet was indeed stirring.

'Impossible!' he muttered to himself, wide-eyed, before hurrying back to where Scarlet lay.

*   *   *

Scarlet's head swam as the circular metal frame to which his wrists and ankles had been clamped spun wildly.

The frame within which Scarlet was spread-eagled was hinged within a second metal hoop, which in turn was hinged within a third. Their complex combined spinning motion was erratic and disorientating.

The dizzying effect was greatly heightened by Scarlet's surroundings – a featureless void, lit by a single painfully bright light.

Scarlet had lost all sense of up or down, left or right, and his stomach lurched as he whirled about. He knew this giant gyroscope-like device was used as an interrogation tool, but he had never expected to find himself restrained within it.

'Why did you try to sabotage Skybase?' Colonel White's insistent voice came from somewhere in the blackness.

'The Mysterons were in control.' Scarlet struggled to clear his head as the frame continued to gyrate. 'It was as if I didn't exist any more.'

'You mean they hypnotized you?'

A new voice came out of the void, Doctor Gold's. 'No, it wasn't hypnosis . . .'

With a sense of enormous relief, Scarlet felt the gyrations begin to slow. As the spinning hoops spiralled to a halt, and Scarlet's dizziness subsided, he saw that twin walkways were extending out of the void on either side of him. Along one of them, Doctor Gold came striding purposefully towards him.

'And I thought you'd want to hear this,' Gold continued, addressing Colonel White, who was approaching along the opposite walkway, accompanied by Captain Blue. 'And I think Scarlet should hear it, too.'

Colonel White looked intrigued. 'Go on, doctor.'

'I've been running tests.' As the doctor spoke, he began to release the clamps by which Scarlet was secured to the circular frame. 'The results are remarkable.'

'Meaning?'

'Basically, this isn't Scarlet.'

Scarlet, flexing his freed wrists, was taken aback. 'What the hell is this?' he said, frowning. Of course he was Scarlet.

'He's an impostor?' The colonel wanted clarification.

'No,' replied Gold.

Captain Blue gave a wry chuckle. 'Doc, you're not making a whole lot of sense.'

'Well, he has Scarlet's DNA. But it's been altered at a subatomic level.'

White was still confused. 'What exactly are you saying?'

'This man has Scarlet's fingerprints, iris configuration and even the rivets in his leg from a break suffered ten years ago. But this isn't the man you sent to Mars.'

Scarlet looked at Doctor Gold incredulously. 'Are you saying I'm some kind of clone?'

Doctor Gold looked up at Scarlet and shook his head. 'A clone is an exact genetic copy. *You* have a unique difference. Your body is genetically retrometabolizing.'

The doctor paused. He could see from Scarlet's expression that the full significance of this revelation was not apparent to him.

'Captain Scarlet,' said the doctor, looking Scarlet straight in the eyes, 'you are virtually indestructible.'

Scarlet didn't recognize the churchyard immediately. The last time he had been there, it had been peaceful and serene, bathed in daylight. Now it was being lashed by a violent downpour of rain, as a terrifying electrical storm raged in the night sky.

With an ear-splitting crash, a bolt of lightning suddenly struck a nearby tree, leaving a smouldering split in its trunk. While Scarlet watched, two familiar hoops of bright green light began to dance across the surface of the wounded trunk, as though beamed from an invisible source.

The green rings slithered down to the foot of the tree and across the rained-drenched grass and graves, until they settled on a gleaming slab of black marble.

Scarlet's pulse quickened as he read the stone's golden inscription:

CONRAD LEFKON
KILLED IN ACTION

There was no doubting it now. This was the graveyard of St Saviour's church, where Scarlet had helped to lay his friend to rest only days before.

And then the voice came again. The terrible alien voice that made Scarlet's blood turn to ice.

'CAPTAIN SCARLET HAS FAILED US. BUT THE MYSTERONS WILL *NOT* FAIL.'

As the green circles danced across the black marble of Conrad's grave, the inhuman voice, unfeasibly deep, continued.

'WE HAVE ANOTHER INSTRUMENT OF DESTRUCTION.'

With a crash like a second lightning strike, a clenched fist smashed through the two-centimetre-thick marble from beneath. The engraved inscription shattered in a shower of black and gold shards.

Captain Scarlet sat bolt upright in his confinement cell, suddenly wide awake. He knew that what he had seen was no delusion or nightmare. He knew Black was back.

Captain Blue stepped out of the lift into the main security foyer. Hailing the guard on duty at the prisoner-surveillance desk, he headed for the executive cell where Scarlet was being held.

It felt odd to be visiting his colleague in prison, but Blue was sure that, after the events of the previous day, it was vital that Scarlet was treated as a security threat. Blue didn't pretend to understand what had happened to his fellow agent. Scarlet had changed since the Mars mission, for sure. And Blue no longer trusted him an inch. As he approached the cell, he drew his laser pistol, flicking it to STUN.

Blue keyed in the access code to the cell's outer doors and, as they hissed apart, stepped inside. The quadrant-shaped cell had a perimeter, where Blue now stood, plus the confinement area itself, enclosed in vertical plasma bars, burning a bright blue. If he touched those, he'd get a nasty shock.

Behind the glowing bars, Scarlet lay on his bed, his back to Blue, apparently asleep.

Keeping his pistol trained on Scarlet with one

hand, Blue took the security remote from his utility belt with the other and clicked the DEACTIVATE button. The plasma bars blinked off.

'Come on, Scarlet. The colonel wants to talk to you again.'

Blue approached Scarlet to rouse him. Scarlet suddenly sprang to life. A quick, well-aimed blow from his right arm sent Blue's laser pistol skittering across the cell floor. As the blow spun Blue round, Scarlet delivered a powerful left-leg kick across his back. He quickly rose from the bed and assumed a combat stance, as Blue stumbled, then turned to face him.

Both men were highly trained in unarmed combat, and the brief fight that followed was fast and furious.

Though Blue was more well-built and muscular, Scarlet's astonishing reactions gave him the edge. Expertly blocking a sequence of attempted punches from Blue, Scarlet managed to throw his opponent off balance. As a fierce, chopping kick sent Blue stumbling towards the bed, Scarlet grabbed the security remote from Blue's utility belt and dived for the perimeter area of the cell.

As Scarlet hit the floor, he twisted round and

Black grabs Scarlet and pulls him to safety.

The incredible Mysteron city materializes on Mars.

Scarlet and Black are chased by the Mysterons.

Destiny remembers Captain Black.

The Mysterons wash over Scarlet's sleeping body.

Now under Mysteron control, Scarlet begins to shut down Skybase.

The only way Blue can stop
Scarlet is to shoot him.

Black, posing as a driver, takes
McGill into a wrecker's yard.

Destiny and Colonel White enter
the United Nations Assembly Hall.

White addresses the United Nations delegates.

Black takes aim and fires.

**Scarlet bursts through the window
in front of Black's bullet.**

The Vampire Squadron joins Black and the Mysterons.

Scarlet fixes the grappling hook to the roof of the truck.

General Zamatev is recruited by
Mysteron Agent Black.

'All I have to do is press this button.'
Black holds up the nuclear device.

pressed the remote's ACTIVATE button. The bright blue plasma bars fizzed into life again. Just in time to give Blue, who had found his feet and was coming back at Scarlet, a jolt of electricity.

Now the prisoner, Blue reeled backwards on to the bed. Scarlet picked himself up and reached for Blue's pistol, lying nearby. Breathless from the fight, he spoke hastily to his dazed friend.

'Adam – Black is alive and under Mysteron control. I've got to stop him.'

Punching the door release, Scarlet rushed from the cell. Blue heard a brief scuffle outside – clearly the guard on duty had tried to stop Scarlet. The familiar hiss of the lift doors told Blue that he'd been unsuccessful.

Thinking quickly, Blue took a Stinger explosive charge from his utility belt and clamped it to the wall panel that concealed the plasma bar electronics. He armed the charge, stepped back and shielded his face. As it detonated with a thud and flash, the plasma bars blinked out and Blue escaped from the cell.

Surprised to find his laser pistol beside the unconscious body of the guard outside, Blue grabbed it and hit the Central Control emergency ComLink button.

'Spectrum is Red!' Blue reported, urgently. 'Captain Scarlet has escaped!'

Scarlet hurried to the Hangar Deck. If he could commandeer one of the Falcon Interceptors, he knew he could get to Black as fast as possible.

Scarlet was far from comfortable with what had just happened. Fighting another agent was not something he took lightly. But if Spectrum was going to keep him locked up, continue to treat him as a potential enemy, he had no option but to escape. The Mysterons had control of Black and he had to be stopped.

Scarlet hurriedly grabbed a flight suit and helmet from the equipment area, changing en route as he took the lift to the main hangar floor. He sprinted across to where one of the Falcons stood at standby and began to activate the automated aircraft-launch mechanisms.

The robotic arms whirred and clanked into motion as one of the Falcons was propelled along its Magna-strip rails into its boarding dock.

Suddenly, Captain Blue burst through the lift doors, gun in hand. Scarlet dived for cover and the robotic mechanisms fell still again.

Captain Blue scanned the hangar, his

outstretched arms expertly tracking his pistol from side to side as he moved across the search area. There was no sign or sound of Scarlet.

'Paul!' Blue continued to stalk his fellow agent, peering beneath the fuselage of the nearby Falcon. 'Scarlet!'

The hangar rang with Blue's shouts, then became silent again.

Suddenly, Scarlet swung down at Blue from above, catching him squarely on the chest with both feet. As Blue fell backwards, his pistol clattered away underneath the Falcon.

Blue was back on his feet in an instant. The two men, unarmed, squared up to one another for a second time.

After a momentary pause, the fight began – a blur of high-speed, high-impact kicks, punches and blocks. Both agents fought with clinical precision and awesome ferocity. Only after taking several hard blows himself did Scarlet manage to plant a vicious roundhouse kick on Blue's jaw, sending him sprawling on to the floor.

As Blue recovered his senses, Scarlet quickly grabbed his flight helmet and slipped it on to his head. As he did so, two security guards, laser pistols drawn, came rushing across the hangar.

Captain Blue picked himself up as Scarlet steadily edged away towards the wall of the hangar.

'You're not going anywhere, Paul,' said Blue, rubbing his jaw. Even Scarlet couldn't get past him *and* two armed guards.

By now, Scarlet had his back against the hangar wall. The section directly behind him was an emergency-exit hatch, opening on to thin air.

Blue saw Scarlet smile wryly at him through the visor of his flight helmet.

'Wrong again, Adam.'

In an instant, Blue and the guards realized Scarlet's intention and hit the deck. As they did so, Scarlet yanked down the emergency hatch's twin release levers.

The hatch opened briefly and Blue clung to the floor as a great rush of air tried to suck him across it. A second later there was a clunk as the hatch automatically closed, and calm again.

Blue got to his feet slowly and looked across to Scarlet . . .

But he had gone.

'You have to stop him Captain Blue. At *all* costs.'

Colonel White's voice came over Blue's helmet headset as the hangar lift raised him, astride his Stallion Raid Bike, into launch position on Flight Deck.

'S-I-G!' confirmed Blue, resolutely.

Only moments had passed since Scarlet had slipped through Blue's fingers and he was confident that on the Raid Bike he could soon catch him. Colonel White's tone made it quite clear that this was to be a no-holds-barred pursuit. Scarlet was a wanted man.

As the extendable wings on top of the Raid Bike's canopy swung up and locked into flight position, the smaller canard wings above the bike's front wheel snapped out. Blue gunned the powerful engine,and let out the clutch.

The bike roared along Skybase's upper surface with awesome acceleration as its twin rear wheels put down phenomenal traction. As it cleared the end of the deck, it plummeted earthwards like a missile.

In the sky below, Scarlet was free-falling fast. As the Earth hurtled up to meet him, he hit the chute release incorporated within his flight suit. A multicoloured parachute billowed open from his back, slowing his fall with a jolt.

Scarlet could see his target landing place in the countryside below – a circle of standing stones on a small hillock. This landmark, Scarlet knew, concealed one of Spectrum's many top-secret Emergency Response Facilities.

Skilfully controlling his fall, he hit the ground only metres from the stone circle, shedding his chute as he sprinted towards it. A two-tiered boulder stood at the centre of the circle. Scarlet leaped on to it, knelt down and pressed a button on his flight-suit wristband. Instantly, the central section of the boulder began to sink, taking Scarlet down into the ground.

*　　*　　*

Captain Blue was in hot pursuit. The Raid Bike was designed with just this type of rapid response in mind, being the only land vehicle in Spectrum's impressive fleet that could be deployed directly from Skybase. Its pressurized canopy, with its attached wings, enabled the bike to dive from Flight Deck and glide to Earth. At the moment of touchdown, it automatically shed its entire flight canopy to become an ordinary motorcycle – though nothing about the bike's hi-tech design or hi-spec performance could fairly be called 'ordinary'.

As Earth zoomed closer and closer, the bike's canopy wings snapped out to three times their original length, giving Blue full control of the speed and direction of his descent.

At the foot of the hillock into which Captain Scarlet had just descended stood a large barn. When Blue swooped down on his final approach, the doors of the barn opened and a sleek red and white car – a Spectrum Cheetah – came roaring out of it, Scarlet at the wheel. A pair of ordinary-looking, five-bar gates automatically dropped into the ground to let the racing Cheetah hurtle past as Scarlet swung it out on to the narrow lane, tyres screeching.

Up above, Blue eased the Raid Bike's dive into a glide, looping round to land, hitting the road only metres behind the speeding car. The bike's flight canopy disengaged, its twin back wheels gripped the road, powering it forward at an impressive velocity.

No agent alive could get more out of a Raid Bike than Captain Blue. Blue was an acknowledged all-round expert when it came to handling Spectrum equipment, or any other military hardware, for that matter. The Svensons had been a military family for generations – Blue's own father, a three-star general, was a military adviser to the US president. There had never been any question about what kind of career Adam would pursue. He had distinguished himself as a student at West Point Military Academy and been awarded a Purple Heart for Bravery during the Global Terrorist Wars. Since joining Spectrum, he had only got better.

Blue flung his bike expertly round one bend after another in the twisting country lane. Scarlet kept ahead of him, matching him for pace in the Cheetah. Spectrum's Rapid-Response four-wheeler could certainly move in his expert hands.

If he couldn't catch Scarlet, Blue would have

to put his Cheetah out of action. As his bike tore along after the Cheetah, Blue flipped the safety cover off a panel of red buttons with his left thumb and let rip with the bike's twin, front-mounted machine-guns.

As Scarlet swerved from side to side on the road ahead, the stream of bullets ricocheted harmlessly off the Cheetah's armour-plated rear shield.

Blue would have to bring on the big guns. Uncovering another set of buttons with his right thumb, he pressed one. A rack of heat-seeking missiles instantly emerged from the right-hand side of the bike. The tail of one of the missiles flared brightly as it ignited and rocketed after the speeding target ahead.

Inside the Cheetah, as he fought to keep the car on the narrow lane, Scarlet saw the incoming missile on his computer-enhanced rear-view display. Even the Cheetah couldn't outrun a missile, he knew.

Scarlet waited until the missile had almost caught the car before hitting a button on the dashboard control console. A cluster of bright flares burst from a flap on the Cheetah's rear right wing. Scarlet flung the car to the left and the missile pursued the decoy flares instead, destroying a roadside billboard as they lured it off-target.

Scarlet breathed more easily. But almost immediately, another hazard presented itself. A slow-moving tractor and trailer were pulling across a crossroads a few hundred metres ahead, blocking it completely. And Scarlet was heading straight for them.

Then, as the Cheetah roared towards the obstacle, Scarlet pulled back a lever and the car's bodywork instantly transformed. Panels in each side flapped down to form gliding wings. The rear shield swung down and the back morphed into a tail fin, exposing powerful boost-jets within the vehicle's rear. When they ignited, the car shot forward. Smaller jump-jets under the Cheetah's front wings fired as it bore down upon the tractor. The entire car took to the air, gliding clear over the top of the tractor and its bewildered driver, before landing smoothly on the tarmac beyond.

Captain Blue's Raid Bike had no such jump-jet technology. In a squeal of burning rubber, Blue managed to bring the bike to a skidding halt, just short of the tractor roadblock.

As he disappointedly watched Scarlet's Cheetah recede into the distance, Blue activated his helmet's communicator.

'Skybase, I've lost him.'

Blue looked across to the road sign at the corner of the crossroads. The arm pointing directly ahead read ST SAVIOUR'S CHURCH.

Blue spoke into his communicator again.

'But I know where he's headed.'

Sure enough, when Blue drew up quietly outside the familiar country church, he found the Cheetah at the roadside and Scarlet standing among the gravestones, lost in contemplation.

Blue dismounted silently, removed his helmet, drew his laser pistol and cautiously approached Scarlet. When he had crept up behind the renegade agent, Blue pressed the muzzle of his pistol firmly into the back of Scarlet's neck.

'Don't move a muscle.'

Scarlet didn't flinch. He seemed transfixed by something on the ground in front of him.

'Adam, come and take a look.'

Careful to keep the pistol in Scarlet's neck, wary of another trick, Blue leaned forward to look over Scarlet's shoulder.

'What on earth . . .?'

In the ground at Scarlet's feet lay the black

55

marble top of Conrad Lefkon's grave. There was a half-metre diameter hole in it and fragments of marble lay scattered all around. Through the hole, Blue could see that the grave was empty.

'Where is he?' he murmured.

Captain Scarlet frowned.

'I wish I knew.'

Chapter 8

Central New York. Night-time. Outside the entrance to a towering office block, above which a giant neon sign glared out the words *Transglobal Transportation*, a large, middle-aged, expensively suited man waited impatiently.

Hank McGill was Transglobal's Chief Executive, a big fish in the corporate world and not a man who was used to being kept waiting.

McGill checked his watch again, then continued to tap his rolled-up newspaper against his leg irritably, beating out the seconds, each one adding to his annoyance.

At last, a sleek, ten-metre long, eight-wheeled limo – McGill's standard ride home – pulled up at the kerb in front of him. A door slid open smoothly and McGill stepped into the luxurious, leather-clad interior.

'You know, I run freight all over this planet.' McGill's voice was artificially calm. 'Everything from space rockets to Christmas cards. And it gets there on time.' His tone suddenly turned to a furious snarl. 'How come I can't get a damn car when I want it?'

As the Transglobal boss directed his wrath at the back of his chauffeur's head, the headlights of a passing vehicle played across the limo's windscreen, momentarily illuminating the driver's face.

It was the face of Captain Black. And his eyes glowed a lurid green.

Black had driven the limo several blocks downtown before his passenger noticed anything unusual. Suddenly, McGill's angry voice broke out again.

'Hey – what is this?' he demanded, peering out at the unfamiliar and deserted neighbourhood through which they were now cruising. 'This isn't my way home, you idiot!'

'This is a short cut.' The chauffeur's voice sounded cold and mocking. He turned and smiled menacingly at McGill. 'I'm cutting short your life.'

As Black used the controls on the dashboard to lock his protesting passenger securely in the rear of the car, the limo pulled up at the wrought-iron gates of a large scrapyard, deserted for the night. A sign on the gates read: *Gentlemen George's Auto Graveyard – Rust in Peace.*

The gates swung open slowly and the limo slid through. Black manoeuvred it between heaps of rusting scrap until he reached the enormous crusher at the yard's centre. Pulling to a stop on the platform between the crusher's vast, pneumatically powered jaws, Black clambered out and went across to where the control box dangled by its cable.

The desperate pounding of McGill's fists against the limo's closed windows was drowned out by the noise of the crusher creaking into action, oil-filled pistons squeezing shut its colossal jaws.

Minutes later, a small cube of compacted metal – all that remained of the limo and Hank McGill – spat out on to the conveyor belt at the side of the crusher.

Black fixed it with a hard stare, his heavy brows furrowed in concentration.

Twin glowing green circles sprang into life on

the cube, moving furtively across its surface. As they did so, strange, green-tinted tendrils of luminous energy began to leak from the compressed cube, swirling and intertwining to gradually weave a familiar shape beside it. The shape of a large man.

As more threads of shimmering green light leaped from the cube, the form and features of the man became steadily more defined, until the flow ceased, the green circles faded and a living, breathing individual stood before Black.

Hank McGill smiled malevolently at the man who had murdered him only moments earlier and his eyes flashed Mysteron green.

Chapter 9

The beam of the Transglobal Transportation truck's powerful headlights fell on the looming perimeter gate ahead. The compound beyond was one of the US Army's most secure – a research centre where top-secret weapons were developed and tested. Its double boundary of impenetrable fencing had been designed to keep out even the most determined intruder.

As the truck approached, the gate in the installation's outer fence slid aside to allow it to pass, immediately slicing shut again behind it. A second gate in the inner fencing also let the truck rumble through, giving it access to the compound and the darkened laboratories. The truck pulled into a delivery bay beside one of the labs, and the bay's security door dropped closed behind it.

Moments later, Captain Black had left the truck's cab and was striding purposefully along a deserted corridor inside the laboratory. Reaching a sealed doorway, he punched a five-digit access code into its keypad lock. The door slid open and Black walked inside.

The lab's interior lights had been switched off for the night, so it was eerily lit by the neon screens and LEDs of numerous pieces of hi-tech research equipment.

Black knew exactly where to find what he had come for. He moved silently to a central console within which were embedded four cylindrical canisters, each giving off a cool blue glow. As Black approached the console, twin circles of bright green light flitted across its surface, as if projected by a pair of roving eyes.

Black gripped the end of one of the canisters, twisted it and pulled, easing the entire canister smoothly from its housing. Now the canister's internal glow turned from blue to red and a warning flashed into life on the console's monitor.

Black lifted the canister to eye level, peered closely at it and smiled cruelly.

Minutes later, the Transglobal truck was exiting

the compound's outer perimeter gate, with Black back at the wheel. As the truck pulled away from the research centre, the night sky around it was suddenly lit bright orange when the main buildings burst into flames. A series of devastating explosions ripped the military facility apart.

Captain Blue stood before the curved desk in Colonel White's Skybase office as Spectrum's Supreme Commander, seated behind it, brought him up to speed with the latest worrying development. Behind the colonel, the glass wall of the circular office offered a spectacular view of Flight Deck and the open sky beyond.

'The installation was involved in military research,' White explained. 'Black's last assignment before Mars was a review of security there.'

'You think he took something from the lab before he blew it up?' asked Blue.

'I think so,' confirmed the colonel. 'The New York FBI are handling the investigation. We've sent a picture of Captain Black and told them he's a terrorist. I want you there to liaise.'

'Yes, Colonel.'

White rose from his chair and turned away from

Blue, pacing towards the window to look out thoughtfully at the view outside.

'I'm due at the United Nations today for an emergency meeting. I'd *like* to tell them this is a war we're winning.'

'Yes, sir – I understand,' replied Blue. Assuming the briefing was over, he made to leave, when the colonel suddenly turned back to face him.

'And take Scarlet with you.'

Captain Blue frowned. 'But – we don't know for sure whose side Scarlet is on.'

'What the Mysterons did to him has left Scarlet with some kind of telepathic link with Black.' White met Blue's sceptical gaze. 'We're not in a position to disregard any advantage we might have.'

A little later, Captain Blue found himself on board a Spectrum Swift as it lifted off from Flight Deck, destined for New York.

The Swift was the ultimate in personnel air transport, an executive jet of the highest technical specification. The cutting-edge aerodynamics of its sleek blue and white fuselage made it a fast, ultra-smooth ride, while its luxurious interior offered unrivalled passenger comfort.

Captain Blue, however, was anything but comfortable. As the Swift soared away from the Spectrum HQ, he scowled across the table that separated him from his sole fellow passenger – Captain Scarlet. Blue had his gun close to hand on the table-top and his eyes firmly fixed on Scarlet. Scarlet, still officially under suspicion, was unarmed.

'Come on, Adam!' Scarlet implored his colleague in exasperation. 'Would I have told you Black was under Mysteron control if they were still running me?'

But Blue's scowl didn't waver. 'All I know,' he growled, 'is you're not the man I knew that went to Mars.'

Scarlet gave a sigh and turned his head to gaze out of the Swift's window.

'I know,' he conceded, watching Skybase disappear into the distance.

On arrival in New York, the two agents disembarked from the Swift and transferred to individual Skyriders for the final cross-city leg of their journey.

The Spectrum Skyrider was the perfect vehicle for urban assignments, enabling an operative to avoid street-level congestion and traffic control by taking to the air. Rather like a hi-tech trike, but with small jet engines in place of rear wheels, and an aerofoil at the front, the Skyrider was fast, agile and versatile.

Blue and Scarlet quickly covered the distance to the FBI building, untroubled by the crowded streets below them. Setting their Skyriders down on the rooftop, they made their way inside to attend their appointment with the Bureau agent heading up the Black investigation.

Agent Avery was middle-aged and rather over-weight, with rolled-up shirt-sleeves and a loos-ened tie. He looked somewhat bemused by the two smartly uniformed, fighting-fit Spectrum agents as they stood before him in his office.

'Welcome to the FBI,' said Avery, rising from his seat to shake their hands in turn. As he sat back down, he noticed Scarlet's empty holster. 'Hey, where's your weapon?'

'Err . . . cutbacks,' Scarlet quipped. 'Blue gets the gun on Fridays.'

The FBI agent raised an eyebrow. 'Yeah – right.'

'How's the investigation going?' asked Blue.

'Slow,' replied Avery. 'But we fed the image of your guy into our Hawk network.' He looked reassuringly at his guests. 'If he's caught by a

CCTV camera anywhere in the US, we'll spot him.'

Little did any of the three men realize that, even as Avery spoke, Captain Black was only a few blocks away.

Chapter 10

Black looked up at the Einstein Building soaring up before him. It was a striking piece of architecture – a simple, stylish column rising skyward to the characteristic transparent spherical bulge at its top. The giant letters U and N on the face of the tower denoted its function as the home of the United Nations Assembly.

Black knew that the main conference hall, where the international delegates would soon be gathering for the day's Security Council meeting, was in the tower-top bulge. Clutching the black holdall that contained the canister he had recently acquired, Black set off towards the base of the skyscraper.

Gaining unauthorized entry to such a security-sensitive site would have presented a major challenge to most would-be intruders, but Black was no ordinary felon. Within fifteen minutes of arriving at the Einstein Building, he was quietly slipping inside a small, darkened storeroom on the top floor.

Putting his holdall down gently, Black crossed to a ventilation grille in the wall and prised apart its horizontal slats with a finger. As planned, the grille gave him an excellent view of the interior of the conference hall below.

Only a handful of the UN delegates – early arrivals for the meeting – were in their seats round the large circular table at the centre of the hall. Black peered down at them, unseen, as another delegate – top Russian military adviser General Zamatev – took his seat.

Black turned back to the darkness of the store-room. Taking the stolen canister quietly from his holdall, he set it down on a tabletop. As he depressed the centre of the canister's lid, six translucent vertical panels in its sides immediately lit up with an icy blue light. One of the sections of casing between the illuminated panels retracted to create an opening at the canister's base, from which a tiny ramp emerged. A miniature, scor-pion-like robot, with six silver metallic legs and a thrashing metal tail, came scuttling out of the canister's glowing interior.

Black picked up the tiny bug between fore-finger and thumb, contemplated its frantically wriggling mechanical limbs briefly, then lifted it to the ventilation grille. He released the cyberbug and it scurried through the grille, down the wall and on to the floor of the conference hall.

The tiny robot rapidly made its way across the hall, unnoticed by the arriving delegates. It headed straight for the chair where General Zamatev sat. Within moments it had reached the general's highly polished black shoes.

The robot tilted its head back and a thin beam of lurid green light sprang from it.

While the strange green light played across his cheek, General Zamatev, unaware, continued making notes as he waited for the remaining council members to arrive.

Within the Einstein Building's large bubble, Colonel White addressed the assembled Security Council delegates. The transparent wall behind provided jaw-dropping views over the urban sprawl of central New York below.

The colonel, flanked by Destiny Angel, was

already well into his speech. Having updated the council on the ongoing Mysteron threat, he was now doing his best to reassure them that the situation, though serious, was nevertheless in hand.

'. . . and Spectrum is ready for anything the Mysterons might throw at us.' White paused briefly.

General Zamatev rose from his chair to interject. His voice was deep, with a distinct Russian burr.

'I'm sure you're right, colonel, but I worry that Skybase is lacking in airpower.'

Destiny breathed in sharply. 'What?' she murmured as the general continued.

'I propose supporting them with a squadron of the latest Vampire fighter jets.'

'Thank you, general.' Colonel White, ever the diplomat, politely acknowledged the general's unexpected – and unrequested – offer of assistance. 'Spectrum needs all the help it can get. Now, to continue . . .'

Zamatev sat back down and White resumed his speech.

Destiny turned to the general and spoke quietly but firmly. 'General, I can assure you that we are quite capable of –'

'Yes, yes, of course,' the general interrupted. 'But you see –'

But Destiny was not about to be fobbed off.

'No, general, I *don't* see.' Her tone, though hushed, was now decidedly angry. 'My Angel pilots are all top guns and our aircraft are the finest in the world!'

'Nevertheless –'

'Excuse me, general.' Destiny spun her chair and rose to leave. 'It's getting very hot in here!' And, throwing the general a last fiery look, she strode out of the auditorium.

Captain Black, watching from above, smirked. General Zamatev, brainwashed by the Mysteronized cyberbug, had played his part perfectly. Black's scheme to destroy Skybase was progressing exactly as planned.

Agent Avery, his phone's receiver pressed against his ear, listened attentively. Then, with a decisive 'Right!', he hung up and looked enthusiastically at Scarlet and Blue.

'We've spotted your man.'

'Where is he?' said Blue, eagerly.

'At the United Nations building.'

Blue looked puzzled. 'What's he doing there?'

The answer dawned on Scarlet. 'He's got to be after Colonel White!'

'Let's get the Skyriders!' urged Blue as they dashed for the door.

As his Spectrum colleagues rushed to their vehicles on the FBI building's rooftop, time was running out for Colonel White.

In his hiding place overlooking the conference hall, Captain Black was busy removing several tubular metallic components from his bag. He slotted and locked them together, one piece at a time. A powerful, telescopic-sighted sniper's rifle took shape in his hands. Snapping the stock into position, Black tried the rifle against his shoulder, squinting through the sight. He could hear Colonel White's voice below.

'The Mysterons have already made one strike against Spectrum. We have no room for complacency.'

Black moved to the ventilation grille, feeding the rifle's barrel silently through its slats.

A few blocks away, Scarlet and Blue tore across the New York skyline, pushing their Skyriders to the limit as they hurtled between the city's skyscrapers, desperate to reach the Security Council meeting in time.

'At the same time,' White continued, 'I do not want to underestimate the readiness of Spectrum. We have superbly equipped, highly trained Special Forces who are ready to engage the enemy . . .'

From his vantage point above, Black centred the hairlines of his gunsight on Spectrum's Supreme Commander. Certain of his aim, Black gently squeezed the rifle's trigger.

In an explosion of shattering glass, Captain Scarlet, astride his speeding Skyrider, burst through the glass window directly behind Colonel White. Launching himself midair from his vehicle, Scarlet dived on to the colonel, sending White sprawling forward as Black's rifle went off with a sharp crack.

Scarlet let out a grunt of pain as he and the colonel dropped to the floor amid a shower of fragmented glass. Then he lay still.

Chapter 11

Unaware of the dramatic scene which had just unfolded, Destiny was heading towards a drink dispenser in the corridor outside the conference hall. She was keen to cool down after her heated exchange with General Zamatev. She knew that she had perhaps spoken hastily, but hell would freeze over before someone – however high ranking – questioned the abilities of her fellow Angel pilots.

She pulled a cup from the dispenser. Just then a door in the opposite wall of the corridor opened quietly. A reflection in the dispenser's highly polished chrome finish caught her eye. Destiny saw a man slip into the corridor.

She froze. It was Conrad.

He hadn't seen her. With her pulse pounding in her ears, Destiny waited until Black had moved a little way down the corridor before following him silently. Black went through the door to the emergency stairwell. Destiny drew her sidearm and followed.

'Stay right there!'

Black had climbed half a dozen steps when Destiny's shout made him stop and turn, slowly.

Gripping her gun with both hands, arms extended, Destiny levelled it at Black's chest. Her eyes betrayed her mixed emotions as she confronted a man identical in appearance to her former boyfriend. Black saw his opportunity.

'Destiny!' Black cautiously took a few steps back down the stairs towards her, arms outstretched, smiling affectionately. 'It's me – Conrad!'

'How I'd like to believe that,' replied Destiny, with feeling.

'Please believe me, sweetheart,' Black pleaded. 'The Mysterons have lost control over me. Just like they did with Scarlet.'

Destiny's eyes narrowed. 'How did you know about Scarlet?'

Black's expression changed to a frown as he

realized his ruse had failed. But by now he was close enough to catch Destiny with a lightning-fast kick which sent the pistol flying from her grip. Black followed up with a fierce blow to her neck and Destiny slumped to the floor, unconscious.

Out on the Einstein Building's rooftop helipad, Captain Blue waited beside his Skyrider for news of Scarlet and White.

Suddenly, Captain Black, gun drawn, burst from the door to the emergency stairwell on the opposite side of the roof and ran to shelter behind the raised housing of one of the clusters of helipad lights.

Blue took cover behind a jutting wall and drew his own weapon. Then, from behind him, he heard the roar of jet engines. A high-speed, rotorless jet-copter, bearing a Transglobal Transportation logo, was approaching fast. As it swooped down towards him, Blue hit the deck.

The jet-copter swung into a low hover over the helipad. Black leaped up and made a dash for it, gun blazing at Captain Blue. Black grabbed the nearer of the copter's landing skids and clung on.

The aircraft spun round and a man sitting in an

open hatch in its side, shouldering a large missile launcher, took aim. His missile scored a direct hit, blowing Blue's Skyrider to smithereens. As fragments of it showered down on Blue, and smoke billowed around him, the jet-copter, with Black dangling from it, roared off across the city.

Black had escaped.

Colonel White, back in the safety of his Skybase office, had good reason to feel that this had been, all things considered, a very bad day.

Admittedly, Captain Scarlet's dramatic entrance had saved him from certain death. But in shielding the colonel from Black's rifle shot, Scarlet had taken the bullet himself.

Back on the Einstein Building rooftop, Colonel White had watched with concern as Agency medics carefully lifted the stretcher with Scarlet's body into a Spectrum Hummingbird helicopter. Once airlifted back to Skybase, Scarlet had been rushed to the Medical Centre, where Doctor Gold was now overseeing his emergency care. White awaited news of Scarlet's progress anxiously.

In addition to this, Black had made a clean getaway, while his assassination attempt had thrown the UN Security Council into disarray. All in all, it added up to a disastrous twenty-four hours.

And now, to make things worse, White's number-one fighter pilot was having a crisis of confidence.

The colonel, seated behind his desk, looked up at Destiny as she stood dejectedly before him. She had explained how Black had duped and then overpowered her, and it was clear that she felt solely responsible for his escape. White had no doubt that Destiny's self-reproach was unmerited, but his efforts to console her had so far proved in vain.

'I had my gun drawn. I could have captured him.' Destiny hung her head. 'But I let him go.'

'Destiny, it wasn't Captain Black. It was a Mysteron. He knew how to get to you.'

'That may be, but I paid attention to my emotions, not my duty.' Destiny paused, then lifted her face to look directly at White. 'I don't believe there's a place for me with the Angels, or Spectrum, colonel.'

White leaned forward on his desk and looked up at Destiny with concern.

'The Angels *need* their leader.'

However, Destiny was resolute.

'Harmony will make a first-class leader, sir.'

Back on Earth, an armoured Russian Air Force personnel carrier was following a lonely road through a mountainous, moonlit landscape. Five crack Russian fighter pilots were in the vehicle, heading for the airbase from which they were to fly their Vampire jets to Skybase. There, they were to begin their new assignment as additional air defence for Spectrum's HQ.

Two of the pilots chatted cheerfully as they played a hand of poker.

'I always dreamed of joining Spectrum,' grinned one of them.

'Me too,' his companion smirked back. 'Their pilots are all babes, man.'

The personnel carrier rumbled on to an elegant suspension bridge spanning a deep, sheer-sided valley. It was part-way across when a massive explosion at the centre of the bridge lit up the night sky with a giant ball of flame. The bridge tore apart and collapsed, sending the personnel carrier plummeting to the canyon floor far below. It burst into flames.

From the darkness nearby, a lone figure

approached the orange glare of the burning wreck. The light of the flames lit up Captain Black's emotionless face as he surveyed his handiwork. General Zamatev had dispatched his pilots exactly as planned, and now they were dead. And ready to serve the Mysteron cause.

As Black watched, five figures, their eyes glowing with an eerie green light, slowly emerged from the smouldering wreckage.

'It's good to have you back, Captain Scarlet.'

Colonel White shook Scarlet's hand firmly, marvelling at his full and rapid recovery. Doctor Gold's incredible claim that Scarlet was now all but indestructible was proving astonishingly accurate.

'Thank you, sir,' replied Scarlet, smiling. He was delighted to be back on duty, his actions at the UN having seemingly dispelled his colleagues' former suspicions.

As if to confirm this, Captain Blue laid one hand on Scarlet's shoulder, handing back his sidearm with the other.

'Here, Paul.' Blue paused awkwardly. 'I'm sorry if I was –'

'Forget it, Adam,' cut in Scarlet, taking the gun gratefully. 'Just bring me up to speed.'

White, Blue and Scarlet quickly gathered round the giant central communications console, where Lieutenant Green was busy pulling up screens of research data.

Green – real name Serena Lewis – was a truly remarkable computer technician. She had once told Scarlet that if it wasn't for failing an International Space Agency medical because of a minor heart condition, she had been all set to follow in her late father's footsteps by becoming an astronaut. Watching her fingers fly across Central Control's complex touch screens, Scarlet found it hard to believe that Green could have been meant for any role but the one she now filled so efficiently.

Green had been with Spectrum since the Agency's early days, transferring from the United Nations Security Development Committee with Colonel White when he had been appointed as head of the new organization. The pair made a formidable team.

The colonel's ultra-intelligent executive officer had been largely responsible for developing the oper-ational systems on which Spectrum's effective functioning depended so heavily. Nobody knew more about the Agency's state-of-the-art computer and communications technology than Lieutenant Green.

As her colleagues watched over her shoulders, Green called up an image of the jet-copter that Black had used for his getaway.

'Black escaped in a Transglobal helicopter. They *claim* it was hijacked.'

The helicopter blinked out to be replaced by a picture of a sixteen-wheeler articulated lorry.

'But there was also a Transglobal truck at the research installation before it was destroyed.'

Blue raised his eyebrows. 'Some coincidence.'

'Well, I hacked into the Transglobal computer – it looks like they've abandoned business and diverted vehicles across the world.'

As she spoke, Green brought up copies of Tranglobal's internal vehicle distribution database records, listing the destinations of all of the company's massive fleet of vehicles.

'I cross-referenced these locations, and they're all –'

'Nuclear power stations,' finished Captain Scarlet, as a world map, dotted with radiation symbols, flashed up on the screen.

Colonel White looked thoughtful.

'Lieutenant Green, where do you think the next shipment will be from?'

'I guestimate –' Green surveyed the on-screen map for a moment, then pointed confidently – 'the Pyrenees.'

In the pale light of dawn, high in the Pyrenean mountains, a Transglobal Transportation truck pulled out of the heavily guarded entrance to the Mont St Jacques nuclear facility and set off along the narrow, winding mountain road.

A short distance away, in the mountains high above the road, a massive silver and black aircraft slowly dropped from the clear sky, using the huge pivoting engines at the tip of its wings to slow its vertical descent. This was an Albatross, the colossus of the Spectrum fleet, used to airlift and deploy land vehicles from the Agency's airborne HQ.

As the Albatross came within twenty metres of the ground, its underside began to unfold, three segmented cargo doors under its belly unfurling to become sturdy landing feet, one at each side and one at the rear.

The massive feet cushioned the impact as the

aircraft touched down. After landing, a platform dropped rapidly from the red-lit interior of the cargo bay. It held a tough-looking, ten-wheeled armoured vehicle. As the platform reached the ground, the vehicle – a Rhino TRU (Tactical-Response Unit) – roared off across the mountain terrain. It's deployment completed, the Albatross immediately took to the sky once more.

The Rhino hurtled down a rocky track, skidding on to the road just behind the Transglobal truck, tailing closely enough to be in the driver's blind spot and remain invisible.

Captain Blue, at the Rhino's controls, had his eyes fixed on the external viewing screens. A sealed armoured vehicle, the Rhino had no windows. Instead, the driver saw the terrain ahead and behind via computer-enhanced displays.

Blue expertly kept the Rhino tucked in behind the truck as it ploughed along the winding mountain road. He stole a glance across at Captain Scarlet, beside him, who was hastily preparing a hand-held grappling gun.

'You know, this is crazy,' said Blue.

Scarlet grinned wryly. 'Next you'll tell me I'm going to get myself killed. Just keep out of his mirrors, OK?'

He hit the release button for the Rhino's overhead access hatch and the roof panel slid smoothly forward, allowing Scarlet to stand upright. His head and shoulders now in the rushing air, Scarlet lifted the grappling gun to his shoulder, took careful aim at the speeding truck ahead, and fired.

The gun's barbed projectile rocketed over the back of the truck's trailer, unreeling a light but ultra-tough cable behind it. Scarlet used the launcher's winch to reel the grappling hook back in a little. It lodged itself in a grille of bars on the truck's upper surface, as planned. Scarlet quickly fixed the launcher to its mounting on the Rhino's roof.

'Winch secured,' confirmed Blue from the cabin.

As the two vehicles continued to move at speed along the winding road, Scarlet fearlessly began to make his way hand over hand, monkey-style, along the cable that now stretched between them. The winch automatically kept the cable taut. Scarlet, moving further and further along it, swung precariously to and fro as the vehicles followed the twisting bends.

In the Rhino, Blue gave a sigh of relief when he saw his friend reach the truck's trailer at last and scramble up on to its roof.

'Retracting winch,' reported Blue, hitting a button.

The grappling hook's barbs disappeared and the winch began to reel the cable rapidly back in.

His part in the ambush over, Blue allowed the Rhino to drop back from the truck just a little, but close enough to remain undetected.

Meanwhile, as Scarlet clung to the roof of the truck's trailer, he slipped a thin, pencil-like device from his utility belt. He activated the miniature laser cutter and a fine glowing beam projected from its tip. Scarlet quickly began to use the hissing beam to burn through the roof panelling. When he completed a circular cut, Scarlet gave the panel a firm blow with his fist. It fell away, creating a man-size entrance hole, and Scarlet quickly lowered himself through.

Dropping into a crouch as he hit the floor, Scarlet looked around the trailer's dim interior. Hundreds of cylindrical metal canisters were stashed in multiple racks along both sides of the trailer. The light coming through the newly created hole was enough to make out the radioactive symbols on the canisters' sides.

The Rhino was parked on a rocky roadside promontory from where it overlooked the Transglobal airfield, a kilometre or so away.

Captain Blue stood with his upper body protruding from the vehicle's roof hatch and lifted his Omni-noculars to his eyes. Adjusting the magnification, he zoomed in on the truck that contained his fellow agent as it made its way across the airfield runway.

A massive Condor air-freighter waited on the tarmac, its loading ramp deployed. The aircraft's vast cargo hold was already crammed with Transglobal trucks, clearly about to be flown to another location.

As Scarlet's truck rumbled up the ramp into the Condor's hold, Blue reported into his communications headset.

'Captain Blue to Skybase. I'm gonna need an airlift.'

In Skybase Central Control, Lieutenant Green received Blue's transmission loud and clear.

'S-I-G, captain – will divert the Albatross to you.'

While Green relayed the relevant coordinates to the Albatross's navigation computer, another alert flashed into life on her giant translucent display screen.

'Colonel, it looks like the Vampire squadron is on its way, sir.'

Colonel White crossed to stand beside Green as she opened a radio channel for him to contact the Russian jets.

'Vampire squadron, this is Colonel White. We have you on radar. Welcome to Skybase. What is your ETA?'

After several seconds' silence, the colonel repeated his message.

'Vampire squadron, I say again, what is your ETA?'

The five jet-fighter icons were moving rapidly towards the centre of the concentric rings of Green's radar display. But still no response came. Green looked up at the colonel anxiously.

'Something's wrong,' said White, frowning. 'Launch the Angels! Condition Red!'

Destiny was in her quarters, packing her personal belongings, when the alarms suddenly blared out.

'This is Central Control.' Lieutenant Green's voice came over the base's intercom as sirens howled and lights flashed. 'Angels, immediate launch. Vampire squadron approaching from the east. Suspect hostile intent.'

Destiny, determined to continue her preparations to leave, forced herself to carry on putting clothes into her suitcase. But as the sirens continued to wail and her every instinct urged her to run to her Falcon, Destiny's will broke. Grabbing her helmet, she dashed from the room, heading for the Hangar Deck.

The other four Angels were already sliding into

their Falcon cockpits as Destiny burst from the lift doors and shouted across to them, 'Wait for me!'

Harmony gave her a hearty thumbs-up sign and a broad grin. Slipping into her cockpit seat, Destiny felt some of the recent gloom lift from her. This was the right decision. This was what she was born to do.

As her Falcon's canopy closed over her, the circular platform on which the aircraft stood rose swiftly to Flight Deck level, rotating so that the Falcon's nose was pointing along the Magna-strip runway.

Out on the deck, a robotic flight controller gave Destiny a second thumbs-up. The sub-zero, low-oxygen atmospheric conditions at 60,000 feet were intolerable for human controllers. Instead, they conducted aircraft launches from inside motion-sensitive booths within Flight Control, having their signals duplicated remotely on Flight Deck by mechanical counterparts.

At the controller's signal, Destiny punched in the ignition code to fire up her jet's twin Halo engines. Another signal – this time the robot dropped to one knee with an arm outstretched, pointing along the runway – and Destiny eased the throttle forward. The Halo jets flared and, in a burst of awesome acceleration, the Falcon rocketed along the runway and into the open sky.

The sleek white planes of Harmony, Rhapsody, Melody and Symphony soared from their respective runways, Destiny taking the lead and the other Angels falling into formation behind her.

Checking her radar, the Angels' leader reported into her helmet headset. 'Skybase from Destiny Angel. I have the Vampires on my radar but they're still not responding. They're flying –' She broke off momentarily as a piercing alarm filled the cockpit and her status display flashed – 'I'm illuminated! I'm under attack!'

Destiny peeled away from the other Angels, desperate to evade the fast-approaching enemy missile that had locked on to her plane. The black Vampire jets fell upon the other Falcons and a terrifying high-speed dogfight began.

The Mysteronized Russian pilots were good. But not as good as the Angels. Melody expertly lured one of the Vampires into the path of Symphony's missile, to claim first blood. Moments later, Harmony got missile lock on a second enemy target, quickly reducing it to a ball of flame.

While her fellow Angels claimed a third and a fourth victim, Destiny was fully occupied with the missile that was rapidly gaining on her. Despite putting the Falcon through some daring evasive manoeuvres, she couldn't shake it off.

As the missile crept ever closer to the speeding Falcon's tail, Destiny opened fire with the jet's rear-mounted machine-guns. A massive explosion engulfed the Falcon as the missile detonated. For an instant, all that appeared to be left of both missile and jet was a giant ball of flame in the blue sky. Then a split second later, Destiny's Falcon burst from the fireball, unharmed.

With the immediate danger passed, Destiny quickly took stock of the situation.

'Angels, report.'

Symphony's voice came back over Destiny's headset.

'All enemy aircraft destroyed, Destiny, except one – he high-tailed it for home. You OK?'

'Couldn't be better.'

'Great. We're returning to base.'

'S-I-G.' Destiny looked down at her radar display. 'I can see your renegade. He must know I'm in range, but he's not taking any evasive action. The pilot must be dead. I'm gonna check it out.'

Colonel White was following all communications back in Central Control.

'Approach with caution, Destiny.'

Destiny pulled alongside the remaining Vampire. It seemed that its pilot had given up all efforts to evade pursuit. He turned to look directly at Destiny, an evil sneer on his face, his eyes glowing Mysteron green. Unbeknown to Destiny, two rings of lurid green light briefly scanned across the side of her Falcon's fuselage.

Then the Vampire swooped away. Destiny's weapons system already had a lock on the enemy jet. She unleashed one of the Falcon's guided missiles, blowing the retreating black jet into a thousand fragments.

'Skybase, all enemy aircraft destroyed. Returning to base.'

Suddenly, Destiny's emergency alarm began to beep frantically again, and a SYSTEMS MALFUNCTION warning flashed up on her status display. When Destiny tried to bring her plane into the correct landing-approach path, the severity of the malfunction became all too apparent.

'Emergency. My controls are jammed.' Panic crept into Destiny's voice. 'I'm locked on to Skybase.'

In Central Control, Colonel White moved swiftly to Green's side at the communications console.

'Harmony, stay within range of Destiny.'

'S-I-G,' confirmed the Angel's second in command as she brought her Falcon in behind Destiny's out-of-control aircraft.

'Destiny, report,' urged Colonel White.

In her Falcon's cockpit, Destiny wrestled hopelessly with the jet's control column. 'Controls still jammed. Impact twenty seconds.'

'Destiny, bail out.'

'Negative. All systems failed. Impact ten seconds.'

White was almost out of options. With only a momentary pause, he took the last remaining one.

'Harmony, shoot her down.'

'Sir?' Harmony's tone clearly betrayed her disbelief.

'I said, shoot her down.'

A second later, only instants before the speeding Falcon's trajectory would have sent it hurtling into Skybase, Destiny's jet exploded in a plume of fire and smoke. Both White and Green turned from the control screen to gaze in distress at the billowing cloud of smoke high above Flight Deck.

There was a momentary hush, then Harmony's voice broke the silence.

'Skybase, that wasn't my missile.'

Colonel White looked away sadly. 'No, Harmony, she self-destructed. She gave her life to save ours.'

Suddenly Green leaped to her feet and pointed. 'Look!'

A white object was visible in the blue sky. Something was coming towards them, at speed.

It was the Falcon's escape pod – the front section of the jet, minus the nose and main fuse-lage, with its own set of small canard wings. Though the pod's engines were clearly not working, and it looked scorched from the explosion, it was nevertheless intact, with Destiny, still alive, inside it.

Green quickly sat down and spun to face the communications console once more, her fingers urgently flying across its controls to scramble the emergency services.

'Crash crews!' the lieutenant's voice rang out over the intercom. 'Escape pod is coming in for crash-landing.'

From the pod, Destiny watched Flight Deck

racing up towards her at an alarming rate, and she wrestled with the controls to try to slow her approach at least a little. The pod hit the runway with a jolt and careered wildly along its length, giving off a shower of sparks and an ear-splitting grinding of protesting metal.

It looked as though the pod would keep on sliding and plummet off the runway's far end, but emergency vehicles tore across the deck and screeched into position there and the battered escape pod shuddered to a final halt.

As Destiny waved enthusiastically at the nearest crash-crew vehicle, its driver reported back spirit-edly to his anxious colleagues. 'I can see her clearly. She's OK!'

Captain Scarlet, in the darkness of the truck's trailer, felt the change of pressure in his ears and guessed that the plane carrying him was losing altitude. Yes – it was coming in to land, he was sure.

But where?

Somewhere that would explain a truckload of nuclear fuel rods, he hoped.

Minutes later, Scarlet felt a distinct jolt as the giant Condor air-freighter touched down. It slowed to a standstill and the sound of its engines died away. Scarlet waited.

Outside, in the bitter night air, Captain Black stood on the runway, ready to oversee the disembarkation of the final load of trucks. The buildings of the Siberian airfield were covered with a layer of snow and the temperature was well below freezing. But Black didn't feel the cold.

Squealing pneumatic pistons forced the entire nose section of the Condor upward, revealing the cargo hold within. Black surveyed the line of waiting trucks.

The plane's loading ramp extended slowly, and the first truck's engine roared into life. When it began to roll down the ramp, Black's expression became thoughtful, as though he were sensing something unseen. He held up his palm and the truck immediately came to an abrupt halt.

Inside the truck's trailer, the sudden stop sent Scarlet staggering. He regained his balance as something small and heavy fell though the hole he had cut earlier in the roof and clattered across the floor towards him.

The object immediately began to hiss, spraying out a cloud of whitish mist. By the time Scarlet realized it was a nerve-gas grenade, he was already slipping into unconsciousness.

Scarlet slowly came round, his blurred vision grad-ually clearing. He shook his throbbing head and tried desperately to reorient himself. It was immediately apparent that he couldn't move – his hands were shackled behind a cold metallic column that pressed into his back.

Looking around, Scarlet quickly took in as much of his unfamiliar surroundings as possible. He appeared to be sitting on the concrete floor of a vast roofless cavern with sheer rock walls, their regular shape and height clearly suggesting a man-made subterranean structure – a mine of some sort. A clear, starry night sky stretched far overhead. The air was bitterly cold.

Far more alarming than the cavern's structure was its contents. Rows of metal racks filled it, rising many metres up the walls. And everywhere Scarlet looked, the racks were stacked with nuclear-fuel rods like the ones he had found in the trailer.

Chains of mining wagons stood on rails which ran along the aisles between the towers of racks. These wagons were also piled high with fuel rods.

A steel-framed shaft containing a cage-lift rose among the racks covering one of the cavern's walls, climbing to the surface far above.

As Scarlet tried to make sense of his whereabouts, a motor suddenly whirred into life and the cage-lift began to drop quickly from the surface. As it reached the cavern floor, across from where Scarlet was bound to the column, the doors clanked open and Captain Black stepped out.

'Conrad!'

Scarlet grasped at the slim chance that he might somehow revive his former friend's human psyche.

However, Black simply scowled at him.

'You know better than anybody that Conrad is dead.'

Scarlet persevered. 'You can beat what the Mysterons did to us, Conrad.'

'Conrad is *dead*.' Black was angry now. 'And soon this whole planet will be destroyed.'

Scarlet surveyed the racks of radioactive canisters around them.

'So, this is what you've been doing with all those fuel rods you've been stealing around the world.' He looked up at Black. 'You've certainly built yourself a big bomb.'

'Big enough to blow your planet in half,' growled Black. 'And there's nothing you can do to stop it.'

He held up a palm-sized silver device which looked like a remote-control unit. A bar of

Mysteron-green light pulsed backwards and forward across its display, and a single red button protruded from its top.

'All I have to do is press this button,' Black sneered.

Behind Black, a long upright metal lever protruded from a boxed mechanism beside the mining-wagon rails. Black turned, grasped the lever and pulled it towards him. A wagon of fuel rods standing on a nearby turntable in the network of rails rotated slowly through ninety degrees, then stopped. A panel in the side of one fuel-rod canister slid open to reveal a blue liquid-crystal display within, reading 10:00 – a ten-minute-delay timer.

Black stooped so that his cruel face was close to Scarlet's, and he held up the remote-control device directly in front of him. A matching blue timer display glowed in its face. Black theatrically pressed the controller's red activation button. There was a beep and the blue digits changed to 09:59.

'There,' said Black, with satisfaction, as the countdown timer continued to register each passing second. 'Now you can watch time run out. Enjoy the show, Scarlet.'

Turning away, Black strode back to the cage-lift. As he ascended swiftly to the surface, Scarlet watched him go, his mind racing. He had less than ten minutes to save the planet.

In the frozen Siberian hills not far from the deserted salt-mine where Black had assembled his monstrous bomb, Captain Blue drove the Rhino swiftly off the Albatross's deployment platform, out on to the snow-covered terrain. Behind him, the giant aircraft took to the sky once more, its massive feet folding beneath its belly as the deployment platform was retracted.

Using the Albatross's powerful radar, Blue had been able to track the Condor freighter, and then Scarlet's truck, to this remote, hostile location. Now he urged the Rhino across the slippery ice and snow at speed, keen to reach Scarlet as quickly as possible, worried that his fellow agent may well be in danger.

*   *   *

The scene at the base of the mine would have done little to reassure him. Scarlet was still seated with his back to the steel column, his hands shackled behind it by a pair of Magneto-cuffs. Around him, sizzling bolts of energy were beginning to leap and arc from one nuclear-fuel rod to another, as the rods became increasingly unstable. The detonation timer read 06:10.

In the minutes since Black's departure, Scarlet had not been idle. His right hand now held the tiny laser-cutter he had used earlier on the trailer's roof. With a little awkward wriggling, Scarlet had managed to retrieve it from his utility belt. As he continued to play the laser's beam on the plasma links that held his handcuffs together, they broke at last and the cuffs fell away.

Scarlet sprang to his feet and dashed for the cage-lift. Around him, the crackle and hum grew louder as the entire mine began to glow with wildly sparking energy.

The lift rapidly climbed to the surface, where Scarlet sprinted out of it, past the fleet of Transglobal trucks parked around the mine's rim and into the open, following Black's fresh footprints.

To his great relief, Scarlet saw Blue's Rhino

racing across the snow towards the mine. As the Rhino pulled alongside him, its side access hatch swung up and a seat slid smoothly out. Scarlet leaped on it and the seat withdrew into the vehicle's cabin, spinning him to face the controls as the side hatch resealed.

Blue was staring at his view screen, puzzled. A flickering, fiery glow was now emanating from the mine, illuminating the night sky.

'What's that light?'

'The end of the world if we don't get that remote control from Captain Black,' answered Scarlet.

Blue quickly swung the Rhino away from the mine. Black was clearly visible against the snow, some distance ahead, striding purposefully up an incline. Then a mammoth monster of a battle-tank, easily ten times the size of the Rhino, rumbled over the crest in front of him and pulled to a shuddering halt.

'A Russian Druzynik!' said Blue, astonished.

The tank looming over Black was the world's heaviest and toughest military vehicle, the pride of the Russian Army. It was propelled by vast twin caterpillar tracks, and a cannon of awesome proportions projected from its colossal central turret. Its entire body was encased in heavy-duty armour-plating.

As the Rhino sped towards the Druzynik, Blue and Scarlet saw a set of steps swing down from the vast vehicle's lower surface and watched Black climb inside.

Moments later, there was a blinding flash when the Russian tank's enormous cannon unleashed a deadly blast, aimed directly at the Rhino. It hit the snow a few metres in front of the Spectrum vehicle, sending it into a chaotic spin.

Blue regained control and immediately resumed their headlong charge, now thoroughly fired-up for a fight.

'I'll teach you to shoot!'

Reaching for the Rhino's weapons buttons on his steering column, Blue released a pair of missiles from the front launchers. Both rocketed straight into the front of the Druzynik, detonating in a giant ball of flame. As it cleared, the battle-tank appeared unscathed.

'It doesn't touch them!' said Scarlet. 'Nothing can touch those things!'

A second powerful blast from the Druzynik's cannon caught the front left side of the speeding Rhino, hurling it into the air. Flipping over completely, it miraculously landed back on its wheels. Despite its ultra-tough design, the Rhino was now distinctly worse for wear, with one of its six rear wheels missing entirely and another badly twisted.

Inside the Rhino, Scarlet, dazed by the impact, tried to clear his head. However, the determined Blue was already preparing to launch another assault.

'Maybe you're gonna blow us all to hell – but *you're* going first!'

Then suddenly Blue felt Scarlet's hand on his arm.

'It's no good Adam. Retreat.'

'What?' Blue turned and frowned at his fellow agent, incredulous.

'Retreat. It's the only thing we can do.'

'No way!' protested Blue. 'If I'm gonna die, I'm gonna die fighting.'

'I said, *retreat*.' This time, Scarlet's voice was firm. And the fact that Scarlet had now drawn his gun and was pointing it directly at his colleague, left Blue in no doubt that he was expected to comply.

With little to lose, Blue remained defiant. 'Or what?' he taunted. 'You're gonna shoot me?'

'Sorry, Adam.'

Switching his gun to STUN, Scarlet fired a short blast at Blue's chest. As Blue, paralysed, fought its tranquillizing effect, his eyes filled with livid realization.

'I was right,' he mumbled. 'You *are* a damn Mysteron!'

Then he slumped forward and fell silent.

Scarlet pressed a button and the Rhino's driving controls swung across to his side of the cabin. Grasping them, he spun the Rhino around and drove away from the Druzynik at full speed.

Within the Russian tank's fortress-like control cabin, a smug-looking Captain Black watched the seconds flick by on his remote control. In a little over a minute, the Earth would be blown into oblivion and his objective accomplished.

Beside him, General Zamatev was watching the retreating Rhino on his display target, revelling in the hunt.

'Run as fast as you like!' he cackled. 'You can't get away.'

The Rhino careered on to a large expanse of ice ahead, the massive tank rumbling after it. Its third cannon blast caught the Rhino square on its rear, causing it to spin to a standstill in a screech of grinding metal, too badly damaged to move any further.

But as Black watched the detonation count-down reach twenty seconds, and the giant tank bore down upon the crippled Rhino, zigzagging fractures appeared in the frozen surface ahead of the battletank. As it rumbled onward, the cracks quickly spread and widened.

Suddenly, an entire section of the flat ice collapsed beneath the tank's weight. With a groan, the Druzynik's left side tipped through the frac-tured surface into the water beneath.

Scarlet watched from the Rhino. It looked like his plan might just work. The flat stretch of ice into the centre of which Scarlet had lured the Druzynik was, as he had guessed, the frozen surface of a lake. The Russian tank's vast mass would be its downfall.

Beside him, Blue was gradually reviving.

'What's happening?' he said, watching the floundering Druzynik rapidly sink further through the ice.

'The ice is always thinnest in the middle of the lake,' explained Scarlet.

Then, as the water flooding into the sinking

Druzynik caused a fatal sequence of short circuits in its complex electronics, the battletank exploded in a gigantic ball of flame. Flying shards of its armour-plating embedded themselves in the ice all around and what was left of the tank slipped slowly into the freezing water.

Nearby, the detonation timer in the salt-mine stopped instantly, its blue liquid-crystal display showing 00:06.

From the wrecked Rhino, Blue and Scarlet watched as the glaring light coming from the mine slowly faded and then died away completely, leaving the cold Siberian night dark and silent once more.

Epilogue

Captain Scarlet was alone in Skybase's Observation Lounge. He sat, as he often did, wondering at the amazing view that the lounge's panoramic glass walls afforded. The events of the last two months had made him realize more than ever how precious the blue and green world far below him was. And how vulnerable.

At the hiss of the lounge's door opening, Scarlet turned, to see Destiny Angel quietly enter. She wore the same subdued, weary expression that had regularly darkened her beautiful features in the days since her boyfriend's death.

Scarlet felt a rush of compassion, the intensity of which took him by surprise. As Destiny took a seat and stared blankly ahead, Scarlet smiled across at her.

'I heard you were leaving.'

Destiny forced a smile. 'Change of plan.'

'I'm glad.'

There was an almost awkward silence.

'Do you think he died in that Druzynik?'

Destiny's blue eyes met Scarlet's as she asked the question that was clearly preoccupying her.

'Conrad?' Scarlet spoke gently. 'No. He died with me on Mars.' He turned back to look out over the clouds again. 'But the Mysteron thing that took his shape – that's still out there, I can feel it.'

And it was true – every fibre in Scarlet's genetically modified body told him the same thing. Black's Mysteron replicant was still alive, still bent on annihilation.

'And one day soon,' he murmured, 'it'll try to destroy us again.'